THE
FLOOD
TALES

THE
FLOOD
TALES

RICHARD MONTE

ILLUSTRATED BY IZHAR COHEN

PAVILION

First published in Great Britain in 2000 by
PAVILION BOOKS LIMITED
London House, Great Eastern Wharf
Parkgate Road, London SW11 4NQ

Text © Richard Monte 2000
Illustrations © Izhar Cohen 2000
Design and layout © Pavilion Books Ltd. 2000
The moral right of the author and illustrator has been asserted
Designed by Nigel Partridge

A CIP catalogue record for this book is available from the British Library.
ISBN 1 86205 211 5

Set in Kennerley Old Style
Colour reproduction by AGP Repro, Hong Kong
Printed and bound in Italy by Giunti, Prato

2 4 6 8 10 9 7 5 3 1

This book can be ordered direct from the publisher. Please contact
the Marketing Department. But try your bookshop first,
www.pavilionbooks.co.uk

CONTENTS

ONE

WOODWORM IN THE CYPRESSES

The yard was strewn with strips of wood and pots of tar. There were tools everywhere: brushes, saws, hammers and nails. Mrs Noah stumbled out of the house carrying a pile of clean washing and tripped over a plank. The linen slipped from her fingers and buried itself in a thick crust of sawdust and grease.

'Noah! clear this mess up!'

Several days earlier Noah had returned from the orchard in a very peculiar mood. His eyes stared out from beneath his silvery brows, as impenetrable as opaque glass beads. A basket of apples dangled from his hand like a coat on a clothes peg.

'They've ripened early this year,' Mrs Noah had remarked, but her husband continued his walk as if no one had spoken.

That night he had called out in his sleep, 'The whole world is drowning!' and in the morning hovered beneath a cloud of unease which broke open when his wife mentioned the nightmare. His mouth dropped open so wide that one might well have been tempted to try and pop a cherry in it!

'I saw God in the orchard the other evening,' he had said, and began to relate a

ridiculous tale about a figure with a white beard who approached him under the apple trees and urged him to build a large sailing vessel because the world was about to be devastated by a raging flood.

Who or what was this figure? An augur, a seer, a philosopher of doom? The word he used was God … a small enigmatic word carrying with it a hard edge like the outline of a lofty tower but at the same time something less distinctive, as if that same tower had no exact dimensions of height or width or depth. Had Noah been duped like a gullible fool? He had gripped the table and spoken of trees, mountains, cities, all being sucked beneath a huge ocean of water which would cascade from the sky. Or was he touched by flattery? Did he glow deep inside when he thought of himself as the last righteous man on earth? What human being is so righteous? Noah was not perfect. He had all the usual faults. He had

a temper too – on still evenings the sound of his voice rung out like a gong as he bellowed at his boys. And on these same evenings he would drink and return home drunker than a lord, swaying and singing raucous songs, eyes bulging like balloons.

If it was flattery it had bitten him deeply, like a winter frost that leaves the grasses anchored stubbornly in the soil. Within days the tool boxes were out, and he went down to the woods with his sons to fell the cypresses.

Was it good for a man of his age to start building ships? He was six hundred years old this year. The body doesn't last for ever. What one might have managed at one hundred was not the same five centuries later. After all, wasn't it the body which registered the passing time: a biological clock ticking away towards death? His back was not as strong as it was in his first century. He put it out carrying a basket of apples this year! And his teeth – they were as yellow as ochre and as holey as a rice sieve. His hair was white and as fine as cotton. His knees creaked like rusty hinges and his eyes were like two misty windows. Was Noah in the right shape to undertake this mission? What was his co-ordination like? or his judgement? Was the brain as sharp after six centuries grappling with life's battles? Who would order an old man to build an ark and navigate uncharted waters?

There was no doubt that the task occupied him by day and night, but if his mind had been a box of bric-à-brac, who knows what odd items would have been rattling around inside it! A dusty book of fears, fat and thumb-marked from over-use. A little pot of dreams tightly sealed except for a slight crack in the lid through which the occasional glimmer of hope could escape. A familiar cocktail of fears and dreams swimming around like a potent gas. What if the green and murky ocean was struck by a sudden storm, split the ark in two and dashed the last remnants of mankind and the animal kingdom for ever? Was this place they would be leaving – this crude civilization, as riddled as it was with vice and error – the only paradise they could ever hope for? How could they hope that anything would be different in the new era? The material was the same – human faults and weaknesses contained in the bodies of Noah and Mrs Noah, their sons and their sons' wives. Animals brimful of brutal passions and desires, equipped to hunt and survive. And the earth – how could that be any different when the water receded? With its storms, earthquakes, volcanoes it would be a violent and unsteady base upon which to construct a home. But there was always the chance that something just might be different and that change might bring paradise – a faint glimmer of hope in a sea of darkness – and Noah clung to the thought as a sea anemone clings to a rock.

Perhaps, in this new Eden, it would take less effort to plant and raise a vineyard of grapes. Perhaps after distilling a barrel of home-made wine and drinking a jar of the stuff, Noah's head might remain full of pleasant light sensations for a little longer and not sink like a rock when he tried to lift it from his bed the following morning. Perhaps he would be able to control his own lusts and desires more easily.

It was not long before Noah's mind had begun to imagine what this great sailing vessel would look like. He had wild colourful dreams of ships with painted flags and gold masts. He crossed oceans on board vessels with strange cargoes: exotic fruits, peculiar timbers, casks of wine. In the mornings he would wake with a feeling of uneasiness. That dream did not fit. He did not deal in fruit, wood or wine. This was not a commercial voyage. It was not to be a common merchant's passage. He was to be in charge of a host of endangered species: the animals and humans of earth, bound for an unknown shore. What would this floating zoo look like?

God had given him the measurements. It was just that Noah never wrote anything down. His memory was atrocious. And now, when Mrs Noah saw him wandering around the garden, he was mumbling to himself:

'500 cubits long, 30 cubits wide, 50 cubits high ... 350 cubits long, 55 cubits wide, 35 cubits high ...'

It was at this moment that his concentration was disturbed by his wife's rather curt demand.

'Noah! clear up that abominable mess in the front yard. I don't know who put this idea of ships into your head, but if I catch him!'

Noah ignored the command. He must settle upon some figures. It was threes and fives in decreasing order. How about 300 cubits long, 50 cubits wide and 30 cubits high? That was it, or if it wasn't it would have to do. Brushing his wife's protests away with a gesture of his hand, he headed off into the woods to find his sons. The roof, he decided, must have a fall of one cubit, there would be a door in the side and three decks – upper, middle, and lower.

The three sons had been chopping more cypress trees. Chips of bark, leaves and round cones were scattered over the ground. Noah picked up an axe, chopped a pile of wood into logs and began rolling them down towards the yard like a man half his age. When he began to cut this batch of wood into shape he noticed a series of small holes bored deep into the grain of each piece.

'Woodworm!' he yelled, so loudly that Mrs Noah was catapulted into the yard shrieking, 'He's cut his thumb off! … He's cut his thumb off!', a cry which only ceased when she found her husband bent over a piece of wood with one eye almost fixed to it, but no sign of any blood.

Noah began shaking it furiously. He had seen this species of woodworm at work before. A particularly voracious creature with an immense appetite for cypress wood. There were holes everywhere but he had no idea how many of them were at work. One, or dozens?

How was he to get them out? He couldn't build his craft with infected material. How long did he have before the rains began?

'Perhaps you'll give this up now,' Mrs Noah hoped.

But Noah was full of ideas. He tried whistling – hoping that a melody might draw the creatures out or lull them to sleep so they might be shaken free. He whistled until his throat and lips were dry and his wife, unable to stand any more, began beating him with a cloth.

He tried reciting poetry – chanting verses like a Hebrew priest – but this only made his wife more irate.

'For goodness sake, Noah! Will you shut up!'

There was only one method left. Fumigation. He burnt a stick of wood and wafted the smoke over the timber like a man trying to drive squatters from a house. The smoke got everywhere. In Noah's eyes, up his wife's nose, in the dog's fur, in his sons' clothes. But still Noah kept wafting. His wife stayed inside with the door shut tight.

He tried log after log. At last he found them. A pair of juicy worms, fat with cypress wood. Noah laughed – now he could fill up the holes and cover them with tar. No sooner had he done that than he made a start on the bigger quest: he took a small resin-coated box and placed the woodworm in it. He had his first pair of animals ready for the voyage.

And amid the hammering and sawing and smoke-filled air, Noah's craft began to take shape as the first drops of water tumbled out of the grey skies overhead.

TWO

THE FATE OF THE BEHEMOTH

The rain was spattering the ground and collecting in pools of muddy water. Noah trudged up the ramp with a pair of fowl under his arms. A cock and a chicken squawking violently at the sight of the dark room ahead.

'There's a couple of lizards down there, Shem,' he shouted at one of his sons who was teasing a canary.

He released the fowl into a cage and sighed. What a month it had been!

Where do you begin when you have been instructed to gather together the male and female of every living creature on earth? The house was the most obvious starting-point. Mrs Noah located a pair of spiders and two mice, but left her husband to remove them. The pigeons in the loft had been caught and two stray cats in the garden. But what a task this was! No sooner had one creature been secured than Noah thought of another. There were boxes and cages everywhere. Owls screeching, monkeys chattering, dogs barking. And that wasn't all. There were different types of the same creature – not just one dog, for example, but hundreds of

different breeds. Red coated, white coated, rough haired, smooth haired, small ears, large ears. He couldn't take them all. What must he include, what must he leave behind?

At night he would lie awake counting the species, turning over in his mind all the birds, beasts and reptiles he could think of. The numbers became unmanageable; his tired mind slipped into dreamland and began creating mythical creatures – fire-breathing monsters, hump-backed sea horses, flying pigs. He woke suddenly.

'The flying pigs! We've forgotten the flying pigs,' he cried out, only to receive a hefty slap from the far side of the bed.

In the daylight there wasn't a moment's rest. Imagine trying to distract a cheetah in the hills and lure its cubs into a net. Then there were the poisonous snakes which had to be clasped tightly around the neck and dragged back in a cloth sack.

'Cubs!' shrieked Mrs Noah, 'stick to cubs!' as her husband released a pair of adult elephants and began repairing the crushed ramp. The small creatures were easy to store – ants, spiders, beetles – but these blundering beasts had to be captured in their infancy. There just wasn't the room – everything had been so badly planned. How long was this journey going to take? Cubs grew rapidly into lumbering adults and they had immense appetites. Would the ark be able to take this increased weight? How much extra grain and meat must be stored on board? Of course they had to take chunks of salted beef and chicken – a slight injustice to the cow and the fowl on deck perhaps – but a lion can't be fed on corn! Practical problems arose daily. The cats were stored too close to the mice and the vermin had to be replaced. A snake reached through its bars and helped itself to an unfortunate piglet which Noah had neglected temporarily as he tended to the rats.

The capturing and loading of the animals was awkward enough, but that was the least of Noah's concerns. This sudden intimacy with the animal kingdom had awakened a curiosity as to their origins. Never before had he appreciated the quantity and variety of the world's creatures. Not only were there differences between animals but also marked differences between species. It was only a thought – and one which hung in Noah's mind like an unripe fruit. He noticed that the shells of tortoises were intricately patterned in diverse shades, that a type of green and brown moth was indistinguishable from a leaf, and that his own family bore some resemblance to a group of chimpanzees.

He paced around the ark peering into boxes and cages, his sandals creaking between each thought. What were the humps of a camel for? Did they have something to do with the desert? Were they like barrels for carrying reserves of water, perhaps – a way of overcoming the intense heat? Why did birds have wings? Wasn't it incredible that an animal could fly and these little flaps of feathers and skin could hoist it far into the sky? Noah looked at his arms and began waving them about. What would it be like to fly – to look down upon the trees and houses? Might he avoid this whole charade if he could remain in the air until the flood was over?

'Stop flapping your arms like that, Noah! What do you think you are – a bird!' Mrs Noah dragged a sack of corn up the ramp and began feeding the chickens.

Noah released his arms. No, he was not a bird. He didn't have wings. He didn't have a hump. He didn't have feathers or fur. He watched Mrs Noah slinging corn at the chickens and reprimanding the screeching monkeys. And he realized that the animal

with the corn bowl was not quite the same as all the other birds, beasts and reptiles on board because that animal with the corn bowl had a far larger brain. What use were feathers or a hump in such a catastrophe as this? What was needed in order to survive a disaster of this magnitude was a powerful mind which could devise a craft that would carry the threatened crew to safer shores.

And what did that make Noah? The arbiter in this game? Was he the tool with which Nature could continue her plan? Was this craft, this piece of his genius, ultimately Nature's scheme to ensure the continuation of life? What was he to do when they landed? What would happen when the flood receded and he had to re-introduce these animals into the wild? Would they find their natural habitats? Would the camel seek out the desert? Would the penguin find the coastal islands?

'Are you going to stand there all day, Noah, with that frown on your forehead, or are you going to get out there and help the boys track down a behemoth!'

Ah! the behemoth. He had almost forgotten. They still hadn't found a cub, and it was such a cumbersome creature. Mrs Noah didn't believe there were any behemoth living in this part of the world.

'Where are we going to get all these creatures from?' she asked despairingly. 'Who knows how big this world is? How can we gather together the animal kingdom? We were just an ordinary family minding our own business until this ridiculous idea entered your head. Look at the boat,' she shrieked. 'How much more can we squeeze on there? What's it going to be like living with all those screeching, howling, smelling animals?'

What concerned Noah was the number of creatures he might not be able to collect. He had already scoured menageries, zoos, local sanctuaries. He became obsessed by the behemoth. Nobody kept them. He asked around, visited markets. 'Ugly, dirty, brutish' was all anyone would say. Noah was frustrated. Weren't all animals ugly, dirty and brutish? No one listened to him.

'There's going to be a flood. Everything will be wiped out. All the markets, cities, everything.'

No one listened. They smiled. It was just another crank. But it had to be admitted trying to save the behemoth from an apocalyptic flood was novel.

Noah returned home. A creature had been caught – a fat behemoth cub. He looked critically at his lads.

'This one's got a fever,' he said, pointing to the white foam-rimmed mouth and turning the animal loose dejectedly. He couldn't risk bringing infected animals on board. What if an epidemic broke out on the journey? Mrs

Noah and a daughter-in-law were packing some bandages, a box of herbs, a feeding bottle. But this was not a hospital or a veterinary practice. How were they going to treat sick animals or cope with unforeseen accidents and premature births?

The more Noah thought about these things, the more they troubled his weary mind. He found himself looking at a cask of wine as if a miraculous solution lay hidden inside it. But that was only an escape. A feeble flight, a poor way out – the path of a weak-willed man. He stood up. He was the arbiter. He must take responsibility. He would manage somehow. But all these strong words had not solved the problem of the behemoth. As the days moved on, Noah realized his final choices must be made. The hunt for the behemoth was aborted, and after much deliberation Noah hoped the future world would forgive him for letting that strange and wonderful creature slip into extinction. After all, there was the hippo, which on closer inspection resembled the behemoth in weight, colour, smell and ugliness. These fat, dirty brown, stinking monsters resembled each other so much that Noah began pondering once more whether the two were in some way related or whether one had grown out of the other. And if this was so, was it not further evidence that the theory about life on earth being of divine origin, created spontaneously by a master planner (the figure in the orchard?), was resting on shaky terrain? On these grounds was it possible that the behemoth might emerge again, or did Nature move onwards, leaving behind her old experiments? The answer was not certain, but the hippopotamus stayed and the behemoth went. Mrs Noah shook her head and in her anxiety saw the behemoth episode as another excuse to scold her husband. And as she belted him with flailing arms and scorned him with blazing eyes, Noah thought he saw his wife mirrored in the orang-utan cage and began disputing the theory of spontaneous creation once more.

To the brutal, instinctive noises – squawks, hoots, howls – that already filled the vessel were added those of the Noah family – the growling of the captain, the shrieking of his wife, the braying of their three sons and the high-pitched cooing of their women.

Noah's thoughts in the days before embarkation were exceptionally muddled. He was pondering on the fate of the sea creatures and how the Leviathan, that monster of the sea, might survive along with the whales,

sharks, dolphins and fishes. He was thinking about cross-breeds which he had left behind – centaurs, mermaids, griffins. Had he consigned all these to myth? He was worried about whether the animals were clean or unclean. How many of each ought he to take?

And in all the confusion everything went blindly up the ramp – into the big wooden house still reeking of pitch. The rain hammered on the roof. The crew and passengers waited. The wind blew, the ramp fell away and the ark door slammed shut.

THREE

THE POLAR HERESY

Noah pulled the bolts across the door and shook his head. He could hear the drops of rain battering against the wood of the ark. He stared at the pitch-lined walls. Light was coming through a window above him. A dim gloomy light, which was all that the overcast skies could afford. On the upper deck he found Mrs Noah leaning out of a hatch, her arm stretched out like a branch, her palm flattened like a leaf in the rain.

'I'm not convinced, Noah,' she said, hearing her husband's sandals tapping along the wooden floor. 'It's not getting much heavier. You've dragged us all into this monstrous prison all because of a little shower.'

A little shower! Noah shook his head again. This wasn't a little shower. It had been raining constantly now for several days. This was the beginning. He was sure of it. It was going to get heavier and heavier. Rivers would swell and burst their banks. Sand dunes and shrub gardens would disappear. Temples, theatres, shops would all be submerged. Entire cities and the highest mountain peaks. Was this clumsy ship a

prison? Was this little wooden shell a jail where the inmates had been deprived of their freedom? Surely it was the other way round. Soon the real dungeons would lie far below them; in the alleyways and corridors of drowned cities; in the suffocated forests and woods of the countryside. Meanwhile, on the abundant and fat seas of the flood, this pitch-soaked vessel would represent the last glimmer of freedom upon the earth.

Noah looked around him. It was important to get used to the idea that they might all be on this ship for a very long time. How long? He didn't know exactly. A flood of this magnitude might rise up overnight like a waterfall bursting across the plains, but it might be months before it began to subside. In the meantime they must be organized, disciplined; bringing on board some of the skills that went into building cities. Freedom, after all, was a strange concept. It only seemed to bring well-being when set within certain limits. Wild, unfettered independence usually broke up into chaos.

In the small room on the upper deck which Noah had turned into a makeshift study and library, he gathered his thoughts on papyrus and clay tablets. Perhaps he would keep a journal, a daily logbook of the voyage. It was here, behind the wooden door marked Ark Library, that the captain could escape from the daily noise and commotion of his nautical environment. Admittedly it was never going to be possible to find absolute silence anywhere on the vessel; he thought he could hear the muffled growl of a lion shuddering through the boards from the deck below; the shrill whine of a hyena; the grunt of a pig; the squawk of a parakeet; these and other noises mingled with the shouts and curses of Mrs Noah, his sons and daughters-in-law, like a badly tuned orchestra. How could there ever

be any peace? When the diurnal rumpus ended as the night sky closed around the ark, the nocturnal animals woke up: bats screeching; cats, with their wide green eyes, prowling and mewing; foxes howling through the bars of their cages. It was impossible to sleep. Noah tossed and turned. His irate wife cursed the day she'd followed him on board. But at night in the dark cabins the crew swallowed their anger. Outside the rain lashed against the wood. No one wanted to be out there.

Noah rose by the morning light. As he doused his face with water in the washroom, he could hear the songs of the bullfinches, chaffinches and canaries, rising melodically from the middle deck. He crept into his study and opened a hatch. The skies were black. Water was pouring out of the heavens. He couldn't see the ground below; it was now entirely covered with water. In the distance he could see water creeping up tree trunks, and beyond them he imagined it splashing through the city, up the steps of ziggurats. Over there was the little country house, the vineyards where he tended his crops and fed the soil, the yard where he had cut and shaped the cypress wood before wheeling it out to this uncultivated patch of land beyond the farm. Soon all this would disappear too.

The intensity of the rain increased so much that even Mrs Noah was beginning to believe her husband might be right. She listened to it rattling against the roof, her emotions churning inside her like a badly digested meal. Was this storm ever going to cease? She was praying for the tempest to subside; to look up at a bright blue sky; to open the huge bolted door and lead her daft husband, her tired sons and in-laws and a troop of wild beasts back into the forests and deserts where they belonged. Was this really a flood? Was the world going to end? She didn't believe for one moment, all this nonsensical business about God; an angry old patriarch in the sky opening trap doors in the clouds and letting water drown the world. If this was a flood, there had to be a more sensible reason, a more rational explanation for it; she didn't know what it was, but there had to be a more plausible explanation.

But never mind the causes. This was a dreadful business, and Mrs Noah shared none of her husband's quiet determination or his smug confidence that, while the world was going under, at least the Noahs and a few chosen animals would survive the catastrophe. The world ending! The beautiful world, that she knew so intimately and loved so dearly, ending! How could it end so abruptly? There was so much out there that she yearned to get back to. Her mind was crammed with colourful pictures of life's little pleasures. Planting seeds in her rock garden, watering them and watching the shoots rise up through the soil and burst open into delicate pink and white petals. Walking a dog through the land beyond the vineyards. Shopping in the city. Filling a basket with rice and nuts; smelling the fish in the market and seeking out the fattest creature for the evening meal. Lingering in the squares with friends. But how could she return now? After all, she had deserted her closest friends. It hadn't been easy telling them. In fact it had been almost impossible. What do you say? Where do you start? 'My husband believes the world is about to be engulfed by an apocalyptic flood …' or, 'My husband, on the advice of God, is building an ark to house my family and some chosen animals to escape …' No, it had just been impossible. So awkward and embarrassing. Questions had been asked. 'What does Mrs Noah want with all those barrels of pitch?' 'I tell you it's that husband of hers. As strange as a desert without sand.' 'Have you heard?

Old Mr N's building a ship to save his family from a world of sin!' It had been too much to bear. How easily friends turned into enemies. But which way was Mrs Noah to turn? Proclaim her husband mad by joining the jeering crowds and laughing as he tacked up his ship of salvation? What if that had broken Noah? To see his wife desert him might really have tumbled him into madness. So Mrs Noah had stuck by him.

What made it worse was that her sons eagerly endorsed the task. It was to be a big adventure. And Noah never appeared to show any chinks of insanity in his calm manner. 'Stay and be damned with the rabble,' he would say, towering above her like a divinity, 'or step on board and be saved.' He could be like this sometimes. Puffed up with religious pomposity. Full of messianic words and, as she might have said (if the Bible had been written at that time), 'biblical phrases'. Such words did

nothing to mend the growing rift between her and her friends. They began to walk past her in the city as if she wasn't there. Their visits to the farm became more infrequent.

It was not the simple thoughts and quiet longings of his wife that troubled Noah, even if her frequent outbursts were peppered with scorn. What worried Noah most, as he tried to connect the flood waters with the figure of old greybeard in the orchard, were the revelations of his second son, Ham. There was something different about Ham. He was the middle child; restless, difficult, always looking as if he longed to find answers. Noah recalled the days when he had broken the news about the ark. He had found Ham already scratching shapes with sticks in the sand; galleys of varying sizes, some with oars, some with sails. It was Ham who had displayed the skills of a craftsman: shaping the wood with the deftness of a carpenter;

piecing it together with the dexterity of a ship-wright; laying out the keel, the ribs; driving in the wedges. It was Ham who made Noah feel uneasy about the tale of the figure in the orchard. There was a coldness in his eyes. Ham was a lover of facts, not poetry. He agreed there might well be a flood. A catastrophe of gigantic proportions. He was aware of his father's seriousness. Noah was over six hundred years old; he must have gained some wisdom in all those years. It had begun to rain. The water was rising. But Ham had seen flash floods, freak storms, heavy downpours before. Was it possible that even over a matter of months they could cover the earth? Was there enough water in the sky? Was it possible to flood the earth by precipitation from the clouds alone? Ham had worked out a better idea. What if somewhere far away from the deserts there were cooler regions; large plateaux of frozen water, icebergs as tall as the snow-capped mountains? What if the earth was heating up and water was pouring out of these arctic regions as the ice melted, swelling rivers and seas, and spreading out over the land?

Noah overheard Ham and Shem talking outside the insect cages. He called them to his study and confronted the younger of the two. Ham stood erect. He was adamant about frozen plateaux, polar regions, melting ice. Noah reached up and pulled the wooden hatch shut.

'Now keep these fantasies to yourself, Ham.'

What worried Noah most was that Ham might be right. But where did God fit into this? Noah hadn't heard anything about overheating and melting ice. The water was supposed to come through the clouds. Perhaps Ham had been overworking. Carrying all those barrels of water and sacks of grain on

29

board had tired him physically. He thought too much anyway, and in a tired body the mind played tricks.

It was not until the night came that the full impact of Ham's theories had seeped into Noah's mind, and he began to feel uneasy. He lay, eyes wide open, listening to the bats at play. Where was all this water coming from? Surely there wasn't enough rain in the skies to produce these vast quantities? So where was it all coming from? And, when the ark began to float across these extended seas, would it reach the edge of the world and fall into an abyss?

All that night Noah lay awake, grappling with these 'unclean thoughts'. Meanwhile, whether by precipitation or melting ice, the waters cascaded over the land. Beyond the din of the ark's assembly, one might have heard the shouts and screams of drowning people, animals robbed of their last breaths, as cities, forests and deserts were submerged. Did anyone knock vainly upon the ark door in those last days, regretting they had not listened to Noah before? For what use was a house when the floods set in? What use were the temples? or the shops and markets? Only a sturdy waterproof vessel, large enough to keep adequate supplies of food on board and still stay afloat, could brave the hostile elements.

Inside that vessel Noah just couldn't rest. What if Ham's thoughts leaked out of the ship? If God's wrath was powerful enough to bring about this flood, how easy it would be for Him to split open this wooden box and finish life on earth completely. Outside, a trawler was swept away by the waves. A family huddled in a fishing boat was dashed against the rocks.

FOUR

DREAMS OF DRY LAND

The divine thunderbolt never struck. The boat rose upon the waters. It felt light underfoot. Noah felt a strange giddiness that spread from his toes up his ankles to his knees. He crept forward gently in his sandals. He gripped the edge of his bunk to steady his body; his face almost touching his wife's hair. Mrs Noah was still asleep. Her eyes were closed and she was murmuring incoherently. Noah would always remember those first feelings of fear and excitement. What did it look like out there? Had they survived? Were they the only ones alive? With a sudden burst of energy he let go of the bunk, tipped forward in his sandals and attempted to walk. No sooner had he tipped forward than he tipped backwards. The roll of the boat sent him reeling. He groaned loudly as his backside hit the deck and his sandals landed on the edge of the bed. Mrs Noah rolled over, looked up and through misty eyes winced at the prostrate figure on the floor; she wiggled her fat finger angrily.

'What the devil are you doing, Noah? Haven't you got used to it yet? Don't come to me if you've done your back in!'

Noah picked himself up and rubbed the base of his spine. That was lucky, he could still walk. He gripped the edge of the bunk again and moved gingerly towards a hatch. He wanted to have a look out there again and see all that water.

A gentle breeze was blowing the waves, and water was lapping up against the sides of the ark. All the way to the edge of the world a flat expanse of water stretched out like a wrinkled skin. The roofs of the temples had gone; the tops of the trees; the peaks of the mountains. Noah hoped the seas would remain calm.

What did it look like from the sky? A single vessel adrift on vast seas. But the ark was much more than this. How to describe it? A box crammed full with the last crumbs of life? A temple, where the last few souls of the human race clung to hopes of salvation? A waterborne city, where animals, humans and a few potted plants attempted to live harmoniously in a confined space? A floating zoo, in which the animal kingdom, including the human species, had been preserved for posterity? Where was it going? Drifting aimlessly across the swollen seas; pulled across the water by gentle sea breezes; following the path of the wind without direction. The captain meanwhile was clinging to the belief that he was directing the human species towards some distant paradise; a shore where human misery, suffering and strife would be banished. But doubts and questions kept crowding in. Perhaps the earth wasn't flat? Perhaps it was circular and revolved through the heavens. How big were those stars in the night sky; those tiny pinheads of light? Where was the earth in all this blackness? A mustard seed swirling through a vast universe; on an unchartered course, to an unknown destination, without a clearly defined purpose?

The ark sat on top of the drowned world like a palace above a crumpling empire, with Noah's study resembling a court, and Noah the ageing monarch, his brow knitted with furrows, his mind besieged by an army of hostile thoughts. Why had this flood spread over the earth? Was there such a thing as divine punishment? Had this been brought on by the wickedness of the human race? Or was it some colossal natural disaster brought on by climatic changes, and the melting of ice at the edges of the world? Noah was confused. How could he believe in God – the work of a divine hand – when these rational thoughts crowded upon his mind; each one sharpened like a spear; stabbing at his old faith and declaring themselves the messengers of truth? And when he leant over the upper deck and stared at his reflection in the water, he shuddered at the thought that this flood might be divine retribution for human sin. Why had he survived? Why had he been chosen? Was he not as flawed as all the drowned carcasses that lay beneath the water? He was not righteous. No symbol of piety. His flaws would fill a library of parchment: drunkenness, anger, faithlessness, gluttony, fornication . . . the scroll would roll on and on. How could he measure himself against the perfection of God? What inheritance could he offer the new world – if there was to be one? Wouldn't it all be the same? Perhaps that was why his mind clung to the idea of a natural disaster. There had been no choice. He was just lucky to survive, and when life began in earnest again, Nature, blind, unseeing, feckless, fickle, merciless, would roll on regardless, giving the human race another brief glimpse of immortality. And so it would go on until she finally outwitted this unruly creature and wiped the crust clean of its menace.

There was a firm knock on the library door.

'Noah! Are you in there?'

The door swung open. Mrs Noah glared into the little wooden room.

'I see; you're just going to sit in here twiddling your thumbs, while the rest of us clean out the cages, feed the animals, sweep the decks ... Do you realize how much work there is to do down there, Noah?'

Noah followed his wife on to the middle deck. He climbed down one of the wooden ladders leading to the platform below. A mop made from a wooden pole and a tangle of animal hairs was thrust into his hand. A bowl of water was placed before his feet. Noah dipped the mop into the water and began to wipe the deck; clearing up mud, loose droppings and bits of straw. At the end of the deck he could see Japheth changing the straw in the lizard cage. Noah was wiping automatically. He was still deep in thought. Would human beings adapt and turn into peaceful, harmonious creatures? Was it possible? Looking at some of these beasts he had on board, wasn't their savagery testament to the fact that a warlike nature was required to survive in the wild?

Mrs Noah was downstairs, too shocked by the thought that the whole world was now under water, to allow herself time to think about the consequences, and the terrible responsibility that weighed upon them all. Instead she immersed herself in work. She couldn't leave this to Noah. He was always too busy thinking. These animals had to be cleaned, fed and watered daily. And she worried too about their welfare. Had they built the cages big enough for some of these large mammals? The lion cubs seemed comfortable now, but how long was this journey going to take? They would grow rapidly within a year. Were the conditions on the ark suitable for each species? She didn't want animals dying from the heat or the cold. They would have to use bowls of cool water and heat from the oven to regulate the temperature. It was all very unsatisfactory. And it distressed Mrs Noah to see the animals caged; they belonged in the wild or, if domesticated, in the fields and gardens around the house. But she contented herself with the thought that had they not been caged and put on board, they would have all been drowned with the other terrestrial species, now under water.

She had chalked up a daily rota of duties and hung the board in the kitchen. Some tasks were clearly more unpleasant than others, and all the crew members had their own particular dislikes. Mrs Japheth would not go near the spiders. She couldn't stand a money spider, let alone a hairy tarantula or a black widow. Dirtying her hands in the pig pen was paradise compared with feeding the arachnids. Shem suffered from hay fever and couldn't go anywhere near the cats. Mrs Ham detested

rats and mice and wouldn't have anything to do with the vermin cages. In general, feeding and watering were far more pleasant tasks than cleaning. Mrs Shem, who on land had taken to the softer things in life – jewellery, fine clothes, dancing – found it hard to reconcile herself to a life spent scooping up piles of foul, stinking excrement and shovelling it into sacks. But it was a necessary job and had to be done daily or the conditions in which the animals lived would deteriorate rapidly.

Noah would have been the first to endorse his wife's passion for cleanliness and order within the animal quarters, had the matter been debated. He knew that diseases spread in dirty conditions and he still harboured a silent fear of the dangers which disease might cause among the crew and cargo. They could not afford deaths. There were just two of every animal on board; a male and a female of each species. If either died before they had reproduced, that would remove another creature from the earth. He worried about his own kind as well, especially his young sons and daughters-in-law. They were the future progenitors of the human kingdom. There might not be much left in old Mrs Noah or himself, but the young ones must be protected. This is why Noah was greatly alarmed when he discovered Mrs Japheth sneezing one morning. He urged her to take to her room, closed the door tight, as if he thought whatever had brought on this sniffle ought to be quarantined, and allowed his wife alone to administer hot food and clean water; partly because Mrs Noah could not be kept away from her sick in-law.

Noah was not pleased to find his wife's accounts of the young woman's condition growing ever more alarming. What started out on the first morning as a reassuring 'Stop fussing, Mr Noah! The girl has a slight cold

and sore head which will heal itself if left alone,' became, by the end of the third day, 'I tell you, Mr Noah, that girl has a fever and we have not got a medicine man on board!' A fever! Noah remonstrated with his wife. He thought she had said it was nothing but a sniffle and a sore head. Now they were dealing in fevers! Without delay Mrs Japheth was hoisted on to the open deck in her night clothes, where Dr Noah prescribed a good dose of 'sunshine and natural air'. 'You fool, she'll catch her death,' an incredulous Mrs Noah barked. Noah was no doctor. The poor girl was dragged back inside.

The rain had ceased. It usually rained in showers now. The sky was full of towering white and grey clouds; nimbuses and cumulo-nimbuses billowing up into the blue heavens. Nobody noticed the sky until Mrs Japheth began to murmur deliriously on her journey down, wiping her hot brow with one set of

fingers, pointing with the other set over old Noah's shoulders to the horizon, the word 'mountain' drooling from her lips. And indeed, had the girl not been in a feverish condition, old Noah might well have believed they had sighted land. Oh, how he wanted to believe it! The mind was so easily tricked. This might have been a real mountain range ahead of them. Dark grey sides. Snow-capped peaks, glinting under the sun. Huge folds of land thrust up through the earth in lofty ranges. As firm and solid as any peak he'd ever seen. But these were just chimeras. He was like the lost man in a desert, tricked by an illusory pool of water. They could sail on and on but they would never reach those mountains. What they were seeing were dark grey and white ghosts of the peaks which lay beneath the sea, mirrors and illusions of that thing which he desired so greatly but could not have – land. If only he could feel the earth beneath his feet. Till the soil, plant vineyards, graze cattle.

And Mrs Noah stared at those clouds too. Was there a city beyond them? A labyrinth of streets and squares decorated with shops and houses? She would walk in the market-place and meet friends. Oh, Mr Noah, these days at sea are so long and tiresome. When will they end?

FIVE

A VEGETARIAN SUPPER

The days seemed to roll on endlessly as the boat bobbed about on the sea. 'How high above the world are we?' said Noah, rasping and coughing as he looked over the sides of the ark, hoping to see another boat appear on the horizon. Mrs Noah was scrubbing the deck with her big hands, in a vigorous endeavour to destroy the bugs which might have caused Mrs Japheth's illness. She dropped her cleaning utensils and began slapping her husband on the back. Noah's coughing fit ended. 'The air above these swollen waters is a little thin ... some-times, Mrs Noah ... I find it difficult to breathe.' He was dangling over the side, staring at the water. Not the clear blue water of a healthy sea; but a thick, dirty water, oozing with brown sludge. Through a wheezing throat he barked: 'Mrs Noah! Cease your scrubbing on deck ... bring your janitorial skills over here at once ... we have flooded these local tides with excrement!'

'Oh dear what a smell! Mr Noah, we've been standing still too long.'

'I can see that, Mrs Noah ... we've not taken enough care over our ablutions ... these brown tides are a threat to the sea life around us …'

The initial shock of finding the waters in the immediate vicinity of the ark contaminated with this foul-smelling effluent had filled them with alarm.

'Muck. Muck. Muck. As far as the eye can see!' he moaned, when in reality the waste was concentrated in a small area around the boat. It had the potential to get worse, but the situation was currently redeemable. Pathos pumped out of Mrs Noah's heart:

'Oh poor little fish! What have we wicked Noahs done?'

The sight of Shem, Ham, Japheth and their respective wives trying to clean the sides of the ark with barrels of good clean drinking water brought Noah to his senses. 'Stop!' he shouted. They couldn't afford to use up the drinking water stocks in this way. How absurd! The water out there couldn't be measured in lakes, let alone buckets. Salty water which was no use for drinking. No! They must simply take this as a warning and be more careful with sewage disposal in future. If there was no wind for a few days they must store all waste on deck in barrels and tip it overboard when the breezes picked up. That way the discharge of waste could be spread over wide areas. The seas would take care of the rest – but only if the distribution was regulated. Too much in one place would lead to localized pollution. How quickly it all built up and clogged the water, until the wind began to blow the ark on and the brown sludge broke up in the moving tides.

Is this, thought Noah, what happens near cities? The accumulated waste of the population is distributed unevenly in the surrounding areas, intoxicating the country-side; seeping into the rivers and the land, until fish begin to die in the stale waters, plants cannot grow in the famished soils. And he began to wonder whether the swollen populations of the cities had played a part in the coming of the flood waters. Perhaps the careless disposal of waste products had altered the natural balance of the land. Perhaps Ham's wild theory of melting ice was not so strange. Who knows what might have happened with Nature out of balance? Was humankind wicked and God revengeful? or was humankind careless and Nature like a machine out of control? When the flood waters receded, would that be a sign of God's mercy, or a signal that the earth was regaining her natural balance with humanity removed? When she had taken back into her crust all those crumbling cities and decaying skeletons, devouring them like some huge animal; and had repopulated the land with trees and plants, and the beasts in the ark had multiplied and were roaming the world again, would

Noah's descendants learn from this catastrophe, build civilizations with care, nurture Eden and live in Paradise? Or would the old cycle of reckless behaviour, which piled greed upon greed, which took from the land and did not give back, catapult nature into another orgy of destruction?

For others the dark seas around the ark presented different problems. Shem could not unclothe and dip his naked body in the water. He loved to swim; but his mother forbade any practice of that sport in such a dirty pool. 'I will not have you fishing either!' she said. She had two objections to fishing. The first was for health reasons: they could not risk eating contaminated fish. The second was based upon more compassionate grounds.

Cooped up with those animals for so long, Mrs Noah was growing fond of the whole kingdom. Why, if she would not kill a dog, should she kill a fish? How could she help a calf into the world one morning and slaughter it the next? Could she nurse a sick lamb back to life with her fingers and carve it up for dinner with her knives? Was it necessary to hunt like a lion when she had large stocks of pulses and vegetables in her storehouse and kitchen? With a firm conviction, Mrs Noah – cook, vet, cleaner, captain's wife, mother of three sons, mother-in-law of three daughters (and holder of countless other titles for which the crew were indebted to her) – announced her decision to prepare the First Vegetarian Supper of this voyage.

A commotion ensued. An uproar loud enough to compete with anything the animals on board had to offer. Noah found the idea of a vegetarian diet agreeable in principle, but unworkable in practice. There were animals being born every day, and if they did not slaughter some of these larger beasts, the ship would surely go down under the increased weight. There were cracks appearing in the woodwork, and it seemed likely that the tunnels bored out of the timbers by the woodworm before embarkation had made some areas of the ship a lot weaker. Whenever the ark creaked, Noah would hold up his arms in despair and cry, 'Brace yourselves! we're all going down,' as if he expected to see the boat split apart and sink. The more weight they carried with them, the more chance there was of disaster.

Ham objected on anatomical grounds. The stomach of a human being, he claimed, was not designed to consume plant foods alone. 'We have developed as omnivores, not herbivores; our digestive systems are not bovine.' It would set off acidic reactions in the gut and could only lead to harm.

Shem's reasons were simply gastronomic. 'Mother! You can't expect me to eat a bowl of leaves. I'm not a rabbit, you know!' He added that all proper meals included a balance of meat and vegetables; by omitting the meat she was upsetting this balance and removing one of the greatest pleasures from his life: the smell and taste of roasted flesh.

'Roasted flesh!' Mrs Noah was adamant. 'It's barbaric. You'd not touch it if I slapped it on your plate raw, dripping with blood. There'll be no more slaughter of animals while I'm in charge of this ship … And you'll see there is more to a vegetarian meal than a bowl of leaves, my boy.' Her voice was raised. 'We'll drink the goats' milk, eat the chickens' eggs … but we won't kill the beasts.' Even Noah – ship's captain, father, tiller of the soil – cowered.

Mrs Noah bustled off into the kitchen, followed by Japheth and two of her daughters-in-law, who quite liked the idea of cooking a vegetarian meal – Mrs Shem having elected to 'keep her hands clean'. While the vegetables were being plucked, the rice boiled, the spices ground, a conversation began between the kitchen staff as to why there was only a single male in the room, and the women lavished praise on young Japheth for making no distinction between men's and women's work and finding himself just as much at home among the pots and pans as among the hammers and nails. They determined to make Noah and his two elder sons wash up the bowls after the meal. Mrs Shem, who rumour had it was calling herself Ms Shem (so as to conceal her marital status) was politely requested to make use of those clean hands of hers. She could either knead the bread dough or work the manure into the soil buckets. Ms Shem chose to help with the loaves.

The steam and smells from the kitchen soon accumulated in such a pleasing manner that even Shem began to wonder what magic his

mother was conjuring up with those old papyrus cookery books of hers. Noah was more concerned with the stove. 'Watch what you're doing with that fire, Mrs Noah! This boat is made of wood, you know!' The wife waved him away as if he were a common fly and, to add colour to his fears, thrust a box of candles into his palms and told him to go and prepare the table.

A banquet was served which would have graced a royal court. There were piles of steaming vegetables, well seasoned and stuffed with peppers and spices, to satisfy even the most carnivorous of tastes; and fresh fruit, plucked from the kitchen shrubbery, where orange and apple trees grew, and clusters of grapes crawled up the walls. King Noah, the three Princes and their Princesses all praised the cook, who was of course Queen Noah, mistress of the cookhouse. But it was not for the meal that this occasion was chiefly remem-

bered (as memorable as that was); it was for the after-supper conversation that took place between the sips of wine as the crew huddled around the candle-lit table; the light flickering through the cracks in the hatches, on that dark night, when only creatures like the moths and bats were up; whilst outside the whole world was silent except for the water lapping against the sides of the boat.

It was Mrs Noah, her head wrapped in a red silk scarf, sitting at one end of the table and bent over her candle like a Hebrew sooth-sayer, who suggested they make up stories describing the fate of animals in the future world. The wine had made their heads cloudy and, mixed with thoughts about the animal kingdom, brought a series of fantastic tales from their lips; all serving to illustrate the many relations between humans and beasts.

Mrs Noah suggested there would be much goodness in the interaction between the two kingdoms. She might have told the tale about a dog who rescues a hapless trekker from the mountain snow, but instead she chose the fable about a blind woman waiting at the gates of a vast city, who is shunned by the populace as she asks for a hand to help her through the winding streets. A dog nuzzles up to her. 'Oh dog!' she says, 'how am I going to get through this dark, dark world?' And, gripping its lead as the dog moves off, she is pulled through the city gates.

No sooner had she finished than everyone clamoured as Mrs Japheth made it known that her comical story was about a multilingual parrot. She told them of a beautiful parrot, caged outside the toilet in a businessman's house, in the heart of a cosmopolitan city, who is spoken to by visiting traders, on their way to pass water. These traders, whose native tongues include Arabic, Hebrew, Assyrian and Egyptian, combine unwittingly to teach the bird to speak the languages of the world.

When the clapping had ceased, it was Noah's turn to speak. He lowered his voice, eager to impress on the crew that not all human dealings with the animal kingdom would be so enriching. He had many harrowing visions in his mind. How the dodo might become extinct. How seals might be clubbed to death and whales turned into pots of oil and soap cakes. How the seas might be fished until they were empty and the catch canned in little tins. But the tale he chose to tell concerned elephants and the ivory trade. He described a man admiring the smooth white ivory of an elephant tusk and imagining all the objects that might be carved from this material: brooches, ornaments, canes. The man's eyes glinted. Would every human being find this substance alluring? Was there a market for it? He could get rich from the sale of

ivory tusks. So the elephant was slaughtered and its tusks removed. But what use were two tusks? He needed lots of them, so thousands of elephants were slaughtered and the tusks made into lifeless figurines and kept on the shelves of connoisseurs, while this unique animal with the long grey trunk could only be found in pictures.

Ham continued this theme of exploitation, with stories about animals used for scientific experiments, including one about a rat used to test medical drugs and cosmetic substances in a room full of sharp knives. His mother and the three young females found this particularly offensive. How could he think human beings would act so callously towards their fellow passengers in this world?

Shem's theme was animals in sport. There was the disgusting tale of a fox hounded to its death by a pack of hunters, and the fur paraded upon a woman's shoulders (which led to apprehensive glances at the various hides and skins hanging from the arms, legs and bodies gathered around the table), and a series of rambling tales about the uses and abuses of horses, which predicted that horses would not only pull ploughs across fields, but carry men into battle, transport people in carts and jump fences for human entertainment.

When the meal was over, Noah, Shem and Ham went on deck, and were discussing the stories as they reeled across it, their heads lightened by wine. Each one of them viewed the ark differently in relation to their tales. Ham saw a laboratory housing animals which could be used for medical science; Shem saw a sports stadium where racing horses, whippets, fighting cocks and pigeons were waiting to compete; Noah saw a sanctuary for endangered species but he didn't get a chance to describe it. 'Pots and pans!' a voice boomed from inside the room. It was Mrs Noah demanding that they make straight for the kitchen, where the utensils were waiting to be cleaned. While they did that, the Japheths, Ms Shem and Mrs Ham finished the last of the wine. Noah's mind was playing around with the stories he had heard; adding and subtracting at random. There were so many ways in which animals were part of the human world. He could see the dragons and monsters of myths and legends, the carved birds in the temple alcoves, the serpents engraved on coins ... He wasn't in the mood for arguing; the quicker he got those dishes done, the sooner he could return to the library.

SIX

SKETCHES OF MOUNT ARARAT

Noah had been spending much of his time in the Ark Library, and at first the others had been mystified by his behaviour. What exactly was he up to? Slipping away after meals in those creaking sandals. Shirking his duties at feeding time and when cages had to be cleaned. Grinding lumps of charcoal in pots of water and sharpening sticks of wood. Humming to himself like a man in the clutches of pleasure. What was that old sailor doing in there?

Noah had been keeping a logbook. This was a surprise to Mrs Noah, whose duties on the farm had included all the paperwork: compiling the accounts and recording the sale and distribution of goods. Noah had never written anything down. Perhaps it was the figures which deterred him. After all, he had not even been too keen on recording the size of the ark, when by a divine spark (or, more likely, rigorous thought) he had conceived of its plan. On board and afloat on those lonely oceans, in the first days when he had set up his study and pinned a plaque to the door, he was glad to find the stack of papyrus leaves on deck. Some had already been used to

sketch out the ark in the days before its construction, but there were enough blank sheets and a few clay tablets.

He began gradually; recording on a day-to-day basis the feelings and sensations he had of being utterly alone in the world, with a few animals and his immediate relations. But as the days piled up and he found himself unsatisfied with the daily routine – the feeding and cleaning, the maintenance work, the endless meals and idle conversations – his entries became more elaborate; his thoughts more complex. He felt an overwhelming desire to record every detail of the journey. He described the weather; chronicled the rising waters (number of flood days – 40; and nights – 40); noted when the heavy rains had ceased, and the number of blue skies. There were details of sick animals; a cat that died giving birth and the euphoria of finding her litter alive. There were tables specifying the quantities of grain and meat required for each animal, and notes recording Noah's fears that there might not be enough beef left and the impending necessity of slaughtering calves (despite Mrs N's sentimental protests) in order to feed the big cats. And there was the continuing battle which Noah fought within himself as he tried to reconcile rational thoughts about the origins of life and the accumulation of the flood waters, with the old beliefs in divine creation and retribution.

His sudden enthusiasm for recording factual details, describing episodes of the voyage in figures and symbols, was growing with every number and letter. The logbook had grown fat. It was like a maturing plant; the words and calculations spreading across the pages like shoots; the first letter a seed. And glimpsing the first edges of the land – the first peaks – he was overjoyed, and determined to fasten those craggy summits on papyrus.

Into Mrs Noah's kitchen garden, where in a series of interconnecting rooms the vegetables and fruits were grown, the spices and herbs stored. Into the 'hothouse', where steam from the boiler kept the Mediterranean fruits alive during the winter months; where Noah gathered the fruit which he required to make his pigments. On his palette, the juices for each colour: Grape Purple; Olive Black; Tomato Red; Lemon Yellow. Into the waste bins to collect the leaves which were squeezed to make Cabbage Green. On to the lower deck, where through a hatch he scraped off the plants which were growing on the sides of the ark: Seaweed Brown and Algae Blue. Into the horse pen to collect the loose hairs to make his brushes. And up the ladders to the upper deck, to the Ark Library where the papyrus sheets awaited.

The ark became a painter's workshop, with eager artists following the captain's example by taking up his palette and brushes.

Ham liked the idea of sketching with vegetable pigments. His pictures of animals from inside the ark, with hatches open to reveal the mountains and the sky, included horses, lizards and bird-eating spiders. Mrs Noah turned her brush on the crew. She did Mrs Japheth's tresses of golden hair in lemon yellow; the dark skins of the sailors in seaweed brown; the captain in his study with Ararat in the background, his grizzled beard in grey. Ms Shem also discovered an enthusiasm for the craft, taking herself along to the birds of paradise, where the lemon yellows, the tomato reds, the grape purples, the cabbage greens, the olive blacks, the seaweed browns and the algae blues could all be used in abundance.

The most recent entries included a collection of animal stories, inspired by the conversation at the vegetarian supper, and an account of the grounding of the ark, which began with Mrs Noah's dream of a shipwreck.

'Wake up, Noah! Wake up! I felt the boat hit rocks. I saw the wood split open. We are drowned! We are drowned! Wake up and save us, you fat snoring monster!'

And there was Noah rudely awakened by his delirious wife, fumbling for his sandals and a robe to cover his rotund belly, already out of bed and expecting to see water gushing into the cabin at any moment.

'Oh snorer save us! save us!'

'Sssh, Mrs Noah! Be quiet, woman.' There was no water spilling into the vessel. But there was a heaviness underfoot and Noah was jumping up and down.

'This is no shipwreck, you mad little woman. The boat has touched land, or land has touched the boat. The seas are down! Mrs Noah, the seas are down!'

Up to a hatch with a candle in one hand.

'What do you see?'

'Nothing. We must wait till dawn.'

Dawn comes. A face at the hatch.

'Mrs Noah, have a look at this. I do believe we're on a mountain.'

And there they were. Nestled on a plateau near the summit of a mountain. Which mountain? Noah crossed the upper deck, surveying the peak from all angles. And when the waters had subsided further, a second peak appeared, slightly lower than the first. Noah was convinced they had landed in Ararat, with the ark lying on Great Ararat, the taller of the two peaks of this giant landmass. He was in his study feverishly recording details; the day of grounding; number of days at sea; appearance of Little Ararat.

'Are you sure this is Ararat, Mr Noah?'

Noah was drawing a map. 'As certain as the Tigris, the Euphrates and the drowned city of Ur lie under those waters to the south.' He concluded from this that the ark had not

SKETCHES OF MOUNT ARARAT

moved far. Had it done so they must surely have landed sooner and in some strange corner of the earth, where there were certainly mountains higher than Ararat.

And there Noah sat, staring out of the hatch, mixing his pigments on wood, and sketching the peak of Great Ararat. He captured the euphoria of seeing the seaweed-brown peak rising out of the algae-blue sea. He imagined the fauna and flora of the mountainside when the waters subsided. Cabbage-green plants; lemon yellow flowers; olive-black birds circling the snow-covered cones and glaciers, that would gather when the winters came. In one picture he sketched the seaweed-brown ark, and in another her shadow in a grey made from diluted black olive juice: an imprint of the ship which might remain when the wooden carcass had rotted away. Then he repainted the ark in olive black, for that was the true colour of this pitch-

soaked shell. He wondered if anyone would find this giant fossil; whether they would be able to date it from the sediment. He sketched the mountain under water and wondered whether the algae-blue sea would leave traces to prove that a flood had risen over the world. He sketched a tomato-red sun hovering over the seaweed-brown mountain with the grey walls of a city in the distance. And in one of his last sketches he drew the mountain in olive black; as an ominous volcanic peak, which suggested that the earth was still the same volatile resting-ground it had been before. A fact which did not please his wife.

'A volcano! Mr Noah, open that door now! and let us get these animals and ourselves to safety.'

Noah explained that the volcano was extinct; they could not run ashore until the waters had subsided further; as they were so high up it would be impractical to climb down; they might just as well make a new beginning from the sides of the mountain when the time was right. And while he began to worry about how they would eventually get down from the mountainside; how the animals would acclimatize to this environment, and whether there would be sufficient regional differences on the mountain itself (from the snow-capped peaks to the mild plains below), to accommodate each species until they eventually spread out over the earth.

Old Noah now found himself doing more and more of the work he had shirked for so long. Laying fresh hay for the camels; cleaning out the pig pen; sweeping the feathers out of the bird cages; collecting stray ants and putting them in boxes; keeping wayward flies off the lions' meat. And as he carried out these practical tasks he thought about leaving the ark. Walking on the land; roaming in the mountains; tilling the fields. And he worried about how he was going to ensure that the animals adapted to their natural habitats. He thought about lions attacking gazelles; penguins dying in the heat; foxes eating sheep; camp fires keeping out predators. The myriad of problems which they would face. How was one man, righteous or unrighteous, supposed to ensure that all these animals would breed successfully in the wild again, repopulate the earth and spread out over its surface? And what was likely to have changed? The lions would growl as fiercely as ever and be at the gazelles as soon as their jaws were powerful enough. The snakes still sank their poisonous fangs into flesh. The owls still ate mice. And, among the humans, would Noah's grandchildren and great-grandchildren be any different? As his descendants repopulated the earth, wouldn't they build cities and fight wars? So Noah shook his head at the sky and asked himself what exactly had been gained by this flood. And when the novelty of drawing pictures with vegetable pigments had worn off, Mrs Noah shook her fist at the old sailor and demanded to know when they would be allowed to leave the ship. She could not wait for Noah to make up his mind – or that God of his to make up his mind for him – for hadn't that invisible old sage of the skies caused enough trouble already? Flooding the world like this and sneaking off behind the clouds without so much as a whisper of explanation ... 'Noah, how can you believe in such a rogue! A shamefaced coward!'

'Ssssh, Mrs N! You'll have us all damned to eternity.'

SEVEN

AN AVIARY OF BITTERSWEET SONGS

Noah was adamant. 'We will not leave the ark until I am certain the waters are low enough.' Husband and wife were among the bird cages. Two songbirds singing out of tune. The raven cage was open and the male missing; the chicks unhatched; the female wrapping her black glossy wings around those eggs, as if she sensed her doom, should Mr Raven not return. Mrs Noah saw all this and laid into old Noah with a beak as sharp as a blade.

'Mr Noah, you dull, overweight, pot-bellied, brown-eyed bullfinch; don't tell me a message floated down from heaven into that wine-soaked old brain of yours.'

Mr Noah tried to defend himself with a mandible as stout as a shield.

'Slow up, old nightingale of a thousand ugly expressions; virago with the icy tongue ...' but his armour soon gave way.

'No, Mr Pigeon Brain. I'll not slow up. One raven wasted on the high seas. The fatherless chicks still unhatched. A mother anxious that her young might not be born alive. And all because Captain Mooncalf fails to think before he acts.'

Back came Noah, raising his voice like a shield hoisted high in the air, to drown that high-pitched wail.

'There's still a chance, Mother Garlic Chops, that magpie, crow, jaybird, raven – call it what you will – has rested on a rocky precipice in this mountain, believing it to be a cliff-top above the high seas. In which case the bird will be only too pleased when Mrs Raven here is duly released.'

'Claptrap! Father Pipe Brain. What is this bird to eat? Thin air! I see it now, drowned upon the cruel tides; black feathers floating on the waves. Dashed against the rocks; a carcass rotting in the sun.'

'Well, drama queen, it's gone and has not come back. So what do you suggest we do?'

It is language that is supposed to distinguish humans from beasts. It is the mark of humanity. The tongue is the pen, the stylus, the wand. Its repertoire vast. But on that after-noon it was not the soft language of love, the quiet melody of peace, which accompanied the merry music of the finches and tits, harmonizing like an orchestra of flutes and piccolos, but the brash staccato rhythms of an argument, peppered as it had been with a myriad of curses, taking as it did the name of the bullfinch and nightingale in vain, soiled as it was with 'pigeon brains', 'mooncalves' and 'garlic chops'.

Mrs Noah went straight to the dove cages, where the birds which she was adamant in calling 'pigeons' had bred in earnest, so that there were already half a dozen or so of these animals pecking about. There would be no danger of the species dying out, should things go wrong. The wife stood with her hands upon her hips staring at the husband. There was not going to be any mishap. Didn't he know anything about pigeons? Doves, Mrs Noah. Well, doves then. What difference did it make? She could tell him a thing or two about pigeons – all right, doves then – she could tell him about the qualities of those little creatures. Had he never noticed them gathering in the city squares, pecking quietly at fruits and seeds and crumbs of stale bread? Their diet was almost vegetarian – they ate the odd snail – but theirs was not the bloated carnivorous diet of the raven. Had he never heard their gentle cooing; their mating calls? Had he never … Noah interrupted, signalling with one hand the pecking of a beak: Yap! yap! yap! Would she ever stop? Was the natural history of the dove going to solve their problems? Certainly he'd seen them in the city squares. Bread crumbs in one end and out the other. All day long. Until you couldn't see the square for dove droppings. What a thankless task that was – cleaning up dove dirt with a bucket and mop. Some people earned their livings doing that. Poor devils! And think of the diseases contained within those grey and white pellets. Children played in those squares. Don't praise the dove …

Mrs Noah broke in again. If he'd just let her finish. If old cloth-ears would just look further than his nose, he would know what remarkable navigational capabilities this bird possessed. Oh yes indeed! Mrs Noah had seen races between these birds. She had witnessed an animal leaving home and seen the very same creature arrive back safely a few days later. The same creature tagged with the little blue ring around its foot. This bird could carry letters; take messages to people in distant countries. This bird, Mr Noah, is very likely to return to the ark, when we let it out of a hatch.

Noah was silent. He hadn't thought of that. A hatch on the upper deck was opened. Noah's palm opened like a flower and the little grey bird flew out into the world.

He watched it until his eyes could see no more above the mountain and the waters. He was thinking about flight again. Why was the animal able to fly? Was it something to do with the weight of the bones or the shape of the feathers? Why could birds fly while humans could not? Birds could soar across mountain ranges, moving their wings with the air currents; humans could only plod across the land, their feet in the sand dunes. It must be something to do with weight. Perhaps the human skeleton weighed more; perhaps it was the brain which weighed the body down. Oh what a world of paradoxes! Here he was, standing still upon the earth, admiring the flight of a small bird as it covered vast distances. But what was that animal thinking on its travels? Here he was, as stationary as a rock, able to picture the bird in his mind; to wonder at its ability to fly through the air. The bird was pulled by the air currents and its wings, sailing across mountains and seas. But Noah's mind! that could look into the seas and heavens. It could puzzle over the creation of the world. Did God create all this like a craftsman, or was Chance mother of creation? What did God look like? If humans had been made in the image of God, then surely if Noah were a camel, he would think of God as a camel. Where had all these animals come from? Were they thoughts in the mind of a creator, or had they developed from small organisms, increasing in complexity as the ages passed? Had there ever been birds as big as whales in the sky? Would human beings ever be able to fly? Could they make a craft like an ark with wings that could take them through the air? No dove, however far it could fly, would have thoughts like these.

Mrs Noah, cleaning out the dove cages, was grappling with thoughts of a more practical nature. She was watching the birds

at cleaning time. Feathers flapping in the waterbath reminded her of the basin in the washroom, where dirty garments were left to soak. Birds perching and ruffling their wings reminded her of the line on the upper deck, where the clothes were hung out to dry. A bird preening its feathers, running its bill over each one, smoothing them, reminded her of the hot pan she ran over the linen to flatten it. In a bill removing dirt she glimpsed Noah's brush; the one he drew across his robes to remove dust particles. Birds must clean their feathers. Humans must clean their clothes.

It was Mrs Noah, the sleeves of her dress rolled back after a morning's washing, who saw the bird return through the hatch. Plucking it from the air in those cumbersome hands of hers, she inspected it rather heavily with her fat digits.

'Anything?' inquired Noah, hurrying down the ladder and seeing his wife mawling the animal, hoping she had found something on the bird to indicate there was life on the plains below the ark.

'Nothing,' Mrs Noah called out. 'Not even a piece of mud caught between its claws.'

'At least it came back,' she continued, while Noah combed the bird's feathers, beak and claws, to satisfy himself that hawk-eyed wife of his had not missed a particle of vegetable growth: a twiglet, a shrublet, a rootlet – in short, anything which could act as a catalyst to raise his sinking spirits …

A week later Mrs Noah, bird in hand, thrust the poor bewildered creature through the hatch a second time.

'Go on bird, off you go. And don't come back without the goods.'

The goods? Mrs Noah, this isn't a bric-à-brac tent. We're not waiting for the creature to bring back ornaments. A pebble would do. A plant would be better. Are we alone, or is there life out there? Oh, Mr Noah, shut up! and let me out of this prison. She waved her husband away with a pink fist. Enough is enough, she was thinking. Yes, she liked animals; her fondness for animals sometimes weighed more than the tenderness she measured out to that snow-bearded old man who had chained himself to her in wedlock. But this unfortunate business had not given her any less work to do; it had tripled it – quadrupled it. Never had she had so many chores to complete in a day. Give her back a small house with a few pets and only her husband to attend. That was enough. Get her away from this ark full of creatures, animal and human. Oh, just get her away!

In this mood, Mrs Noah, exhausted, tired, overworked, done over, cracking at the seams of her dress, retired to the upper deck and sat with Mrs or, more correctly, Ms Shem.

'Drop the r, mother,' that champion of women's liberty was saying to her mother-in-law. For she believed that a woman who went by the title of Mrs was nothing more than the servant of the Mr she had married.

'The Mr is the male part. When we add the s to it, we are admitting to being the servant of that man.' She believed that, by removing the r, a woman could become master of herself – the M for madam. As much as this revelation interested Mrs Noah – and she admitted to liking the idea – she decided she could never get used to 'Ms Noah'. Anyway it wouldn't cut down her tasks. This angered Ms Shem, who accused her of wilfully accepting a life committed to scrubbing Noah's smelly sandals and darning his damn socks! Ms Shem concluded that for all her militant protests, her mother-in-law was rather conventional at the core of her spirit, and wished she was more like Ms Ham, who had adopted the feminist title with the belief that it was the

first stage on the road to independence.

Mrs Noah's spirits were greatly revived and enlivened by the news her husband brought up that evening. The dove was back again. Noah pulled his arm from behind his back and, holding an olive leaf between thumb and forefinger, dangled the blade beneath his wife's nose. Oh how delighted Mrs Noah was to see that peaceful little leaf shining like an emerald beneath her nostrils. The entire crew were delighted. Embarkation loomed. Not yet! said Noah, standing back. Better to be wholly safe than woefully sorry. They would wait a further seven days and try the bird again. Cries; shouts of discontent; an oath or two; long looks at the bolted door; black looks at the bull-headed captain.

But what a week it would prove to be. For the captain it was a week of a hundred questions. Our skins are very dark. Is this because we have lived our lives where the earth is hot? Will our descendants move out towards cooler regions and turn white? Will the white-skinned tribes fight the black-skinned tribes? Do the skins of animals change according to where they settle? How many days will it take to disperse this ramshackle zoo? Will the deaths of any animals and ultimate extinctions be charged to the Noah account, and have to be settled by penance before the death of the aforementioned Noah family? How many burials will have to be made when the bodies of drowned men and women are washed up on the plains? Will the ark's captain live to see the world prosper again? Is wishing for more than six centenaries and one, a wilful act of greed, in a world where few have seen out the first century, let alone six? Will our descendants be weakened through interbreeding?

For the captain's wife (and crew) it was a

week of a hundred tasks. Scrub decks – leave ark in the condition it was entered. Scrub clothes – enter the spotless new world in clean linen. Scrub anything which looks dirty. List animals on board, with quantities. Categorize into mammals, reptiles and insects. Tie up Noah's beak with a cloth – for he thinks too many thoughts and asks too many questions.

On day seven the bird did not return. The quarrelling ceased. The bickering ended; and the stiff and rusty bolts that fastened the ark door squeaked as they were pushed back.

EIGHT

SPLITTING THE RAINBOW

Feet which had stalked the bare boards of the ark for so long were pressed upon the damp earth of the mountain. First Noah, pushing his hooves through the leather of his sandals and touching the soil. Then Mrs Noah, squashing her trotters into the land and leaping with glee. Then the Shems, Hams and Japheths, squeezing their claws against the earth with equal rapture.

The animals didn't file out two by two. An ant might have crawled into the world. A worm might have burrowed through the wood where the pitch was wearing thin. But how were the tigers and elephants, the lizards and turtles, the ravens and owls, to escape from their cells? Had the cages been opened simultaneously and the animals left to their own devices, the lions would have eaten the deer, the snakes would have eaten the rabbits, the spiders would have eaten the flies. To prevent the inhabitants of the ark becoming one long food chain with no room for renewing links, the animals were distributed carefully cage by cage, placed in the habitat most closely resembling their natural environment and left to breed and spread across the world. Some had given birth on the

ark, and their progeny increased their chance of survival in the wild. Others were given the greatest chance of survival by placing them as far away as possible from their predators. Naturally there had to be compromises. Noah noticed a lion feeding her cubs with rabbit meat, for the rabbits were more plentiful than deer. The penguins began a colony on the edge of a glacier which developed on Ararat in the winter months and gradually made their way south to coastal islands. It would be a delight each day to notice new birds in the trees and skies, to go on long walks and find elephants and rhinos on the plains. Of course Noah would never know exactly what had survived and what hadn't. There were animals in the waters, the deserts, the forests – this would have to do. Nature would now have to take her course. Noah had the plantation to tend, the huts to finish and a duty to carry out in the forest.

Mrs Noah was peeling some potatoes one afternoon, hoping to recreate the first vegetarian meal on land, when a rather nasty burning smell reached her nostrils. Fearing the hut was on fire, she dropped her peeling utensils (and the potato she was holding), rushed outside and surveyed the shelter from tip to toe. Nothing. Not even a spark. Shem shook his head and carried on tapping at the wood. But the smell of burning was stronger than ever. Turning towards the plantations, she noticed a thin column of smoke rising up through the trees. Noah! she said to herself and, wiping her hands on a cloth apron, prepared to do battle.

What a sight greeted her in the clearing! A fat little man in sandals stoking a small fire with a stick; and over a grate a pile of smouldering carcasses. He was a menace, a grub (no, that would be an injustice to the grub), a fiend, a scoundrel! No sooner was he out of the ark

than he was poking Nature in the ribs again. Mastering her, moulding her, mauling her with his spiteful paws; starting presumably as he meant to go on. Before her husband had time to defend himself Mrs Noah lunged at him and grabbed the stick.

'For the love of Lucifer! What the devil are you playing at?'

Noah looked bewildered and tried to explain that he was offering a sacrifice to please God.

'A sacrifice to please God! You sacrifice your own fat carcass ... the devil take you.'

Mrs Noah was hoisting the burning car-casses off the fire. She poked Noah in the ribs with the stick.

'How many days have we been at sea try-ing to nurture these animals? The devil take you and your God! Oh those poor little lambs. Oh look, there are even birds here, and you've had a rabbit ...'

Noah, shorn of his stick and fire, looked rather meek. He was scratching his beard and bits of ash were falling from it. He had no answers for his wife. He hadn't thought about his actions. Wasn't it traditional to make a sacrifice before God to offer thanks for saving the ark? But Mrs Noah was boiling.

'That's right, blame someone else for your actions ... a six hundred-year-old child, that's what you are.'

She was poking the smoking meat.

'Where is He then? I'll give Him a piece of my mind. Never showed His face once, has He? Stalking in the background somewhere, always invisible. What's He doing? Holding a barbecue? Intoxicating Himself with the smell of cooking lamb's flesh?'

Noah stood still. She hadn't finished yet. Even God would find it hard to defend Himself against this onslaught.

'How can you bow down before a brute

like that? The devil take your lord of the skies. Give me a God who is the sap oozing through a blade of grass, the blood pumping in our veins, the water babbling through a brook. Give me a God who resides within the creatures and plants which crawl over the earth; who can be a stream in spring, a flower in summer, a leaf in autumn, a snowflake in winter. And if you can't give me this … put Mrs God on the throne and topple that bumbling patriarch, that old tyrant, that God who was made in the image of man, who would rather smell the odour of a burning lamb than hear it bleating in a field.'

Mrs Noah soon regretted this outburst. It appeared to send Noah off balance again. It was as if he was back in the orchard in the days when he had a vision of the flood. The wine didn't help. She worried about him. Up there in the deserted shell of the ark, his silhouette weaving backwards and forwards.

Conducting conversations with himself. Oh, she was so worried. Ham, who was using the old study as a base from which to examine the skies at various times of the day and night, had heard his father pacing around the lower decks, asking strange questions.

'So we must be fruitful and increase and swarm all over the land … but there must be limits, surely? How many people can the earth sustain?

'Look out of that hatch. What do you see? Valleys, hills? Go down there and look around. Pick your way through the bones and bricks. The dead men and women. The crumbling cities. We were fruitful before and we swarmed all over the earth, building our temples and ploughing our fields. Slaughtering the very same beasts which you now give into our hands, their eyes full of the same fear. We ruled over the earth before, and the result was catastrophe, flooding, devastation of the soil.

Won't it be the same again?

'When the land is teeming with humans again. When they are cutting down trees and building ships greater than this ark. When they are turning whole forests into fleets and fighting each other over the precious metals that lie within the earth's crust, will you punish them again for their wickedness?

'Why put a fancy bow in the sky? Why make a covenant with creatures who will continue to pillage the earth? Why give us authority over the animals? Are humans any more important than other life forms in this world?'

On hearing this, Ham approached his father – who smelt strongly of wine – ushering his parent into the study, where Noah had spent so much of the journey, he pointed to a rainbow that arched over Ararat.

'Now look at this,' said Ham. Taking a fragment of crystal which he had found on the mountainside, he placed it on a piece of papyrus that lay in the sunlight. 'There!' said Ham triumphantly, and pointed to the little rainbow which had appeared on the papyrus leaf. Noah was astonished. He had been drinking too much. It was the wine. How else could this miracle have occurred? Ham shook his head. What miracle? And he tried to explain to his superstitious old father that he had noticed that every time there was a shower while the sun was shining, a bow appeared in the clouds. Every time he held the crystal under the sun he could make a bow on the papyrus. He thought in some way the water droplets and the crystals could split up the sun's light. Light was not golden yellow or orange red like the sun, but a mixture of colours – those that could be seen in the rainbow – red, orange, yellow, green, blue, indigo and violet. This was all too much for Noah. Couldn't anything in this world be explained with reference to God? Ham escorted him back to the hut. His father was too drunk to take any more in. 'No, Father Noah, I don't think there's a bag of gold at the end of it,' said Mrs Japheth, closing his door.

Noah remembered waking the following morning with a sore head, but in a more sober mood watched his son demonstrate the experiment again. And there it was – the rainbow on the papyrus. He needed time; a little space of his own to try and make sense of it all. He felt different. When you'd saved the world, farm work suddenly looked rather dull. How had he stood six centuries of it! These would be his days of luxury and ease. He had just saved the world. Didn't he deserve some reward? Yet he ought to till the soil. It gave meaning to his life. The land used to be something solid he had held on to. Everything seemed to be breaking apart.

He was lying under an apple tree at the edge of his orchard. The sky was an azure blue with little puffs of white cloud, like the shell of a bird's egg. He was sipping from his wine flask again and turning the leaves of his logbook. Here it was, a detailed record of the voyage. If anyone didn't believe him they just had to read this log. He lay back and rested his swirling head against a trunk, playing tricks upon himself; imagining he was in the orchard in the days before the flood, in lands south of Ararat; when he thought he had first seen God.

Perhaps the flood was a dream from which he was just waking. A little ship in his mind taking shape in the cypress forests; the shadow of a behemoth; seas swollen by melting ice and heavy rain; clouds which looked like mountains; Mrs Noah cooking a vegetarian supper; images of Mount Ararat; a quarrel in the aviary; Ham splitting up the rainbow with his crystal. But if this was all a dream, why could he feel the shadow of the ark upon his back as it blocked out the sun? Why, when he looked up through the apple trees, could he see the dark shell of that vessel sitting high up on the peak, with birds already nesting in its hull?

Perhaps it had happened, but everything had been exaggerated in his mind. Perhaps the seas which he thought had covered the earth were only local tides. Perhaps the ark was only a fishing boat and the animals on board only the livestock he had kept on his old farm. Perhaps his mind had tricked him into believing a cat was a lion; a dog was a hyena; a chicken was an ostrich; a cow was a hippopotamus; a worm was a snake. How could he have gathered up so many animals and taken them on board? Had he been tricked? Did the world stretch beyond the waters he had sailed? Had he saved the world, or just his own family and livestock? It had all

seemed so clear. So real. And yet now that it was all over, the events seemed more illusory; more like a dream. He had built an ark. He had sailed the seas and kept a log. Surely he had done all this?

Suddenly Noah wanted it all to be true. He wanted it exaggerated. He wanted to be the immortal hero who had saved the world from destruction. He would live beyond a thousand years. His story would live on in religious books. It might get changed – these things always did with time. But the essentials would be there. Noah, the righteous man who followed God's command and saved the world. Noah clung to these thoughts like a man gripping rocks which are breaking away from a precipice. Why could he no longer see the shadow of the ark? Why did Ararat look like a small hillock? Why did the log feel like a lump of wrinkled tree bark? Where had the rainbow gone, and why did it look like all the

rainbows he had ever seen? Were those figures approaching the orchard Mrs Noah and his sons, or his wife and her friends? Were those voices telling him to come and help finish building the huts, or mocking him for sitting in the land of Nod and dreaming of a flood and a ship floating above a sunken world?